This Book Belongs To

_____

_____

Storybook
HEIRLOOMS

PRESENTS

Chantelle and the School Play

Written by Judith Marie Austin

Illustrated by Virginia Kylberg

FOUR

Christmas was coming and Chantelle was very excited. Today her principal would announce the parts for the school Christmas Play.

Chantelle wanted to be the Christmas Angel. Whoever played the Christmas Angel would wear the long golden wings and the sparkly halo...

Best of all, whoever played the Christmas Angel didn't have to sing.

If Chantelle couldn't be the Christmas Angel, she decided she might like to play Rudolph the Red-Nosed Reindeer. Or maybe she could be Frosty the Snowman with the button nose...

Best of all, Chantelle thought, Rudolph and Frosty didn't have to sing.

Chantelle would even be happy to play one of the Christmas Bells because the Christmas Bells all wore big red bows with long trailing ribbons...

But best of all, Chantelle knew, even though the Christmas Bells *did* have to chime, they *didn't* have to sing. Chantelle sat up straighter as her school principal called for attention.

*T*hank you for being so patient," Mrs. Barnsworth said. "I know you've all been very anxious to learn which part you will play in our annual Christmas program."

An expectant hush fell.

"Bobby, you will play Frosty this year," Mrs. Barnsworth announced, reading from a very long list. "And Cindy, you will be Rudolph."

Chantelle held her breath as Mrs. Barnsworth named all twenty Christmas Bells, letting it out in a big whoosh of disappointment when she wasn't named among them.

"And Savannah, you will be our Christmas Angel." Savannah was Chantelle's best friend, and even though she was very happy for her, she was getting a little worried.

"Now for this year's Elves," Mrs. Barnsworth said. "Nicky, Susan, Tommy..."

Chantelle did not want to play an Elf. The Elves were a chorus and they all had to sing. Maybe, just maybe, Chantelle thought glumly, she could stand in the back and nobody would know that she wasn't really singing.

She was thinking so hard that she forgot to listen, and when she looked up, Mrs. Barnsworth was calling out the last of the names, "...Cathy and David. And Lindsey."

Chantelle had missed her name! Reaching over, she tugged on Savannah's sleeve. "Savannah," she whispered, "do I have to be...?"

"Chantelle?" Mrs. Barnsworth called. "Chantelle, I haven't forgotten you. This year, you will be our Sugar Plum Princess."

The Sugar Plum Princess! *Oh no, not the Sugar Plum Princess!*

The Sugar Plum Princess was the lead role! Everyone would be looking at her! And the Sugar Plum Princess had dozens of lines, maybe even *hundreds* of lines, to memorize!

And worst of all, oh, much, much worse! The Sugar Plum Princess had to *SING!*

hantelle walked home with Savannah after school, kicking through piles of crunchy brown leaves. Savannah was chattering happily about the Christmas Play. Chantelle still couldn't quite believe her incredibly bad luck.

Maybe I'll catch a cold, she thought. Or, maybe we'll have a blizzard. Or, maybe, *just maybe,* when they hear me sing, they will decide they don't want me to be the Sugar Plum Princess after all.

When she got home, she dropped her book bag on the front porch, circled around the side of the house, and went straight to the backyard gazebo. Her squirrel friend, Miss Sassy Tail, was busily burying yet another acorn beneath the wide steps. "Oh, it's you," she said, her feathery tail twitching furiously. "You're home from school early. No playing in the playground today?"

"I didn't feel like playing," Chantelle said, climbing up on the seat. She was staring sadly at the old gnarled maple tree next to the gazebo.

"Something wrong?" Sir Hops-A-Lot hopped over, his tall bunny ears quivering with concern.

NINE

verything's wrong," Chantelle said, scooting over on the seat to make more room for Miss Sassy Tail.

"Oh, dear," the squirrel murmured as she scampered up. "Is there anything we can do?"

"How would you like to be the Sugar Plum Princess in the Christmas Play?"

"Sugar? Plums? Mmmmmmhhrrr, mmrrr," Rusty Raccoon yawned from the hollow of the tree. "Sounds tasty."

"Not real sugar plums," Chantelle explained to the sleepy raccoon. "It is the lead role in the Christmas Play. Sorry we woke you," she apologized, leaning out to brush a dried leaf from his bushy, striped tail. "I'm kind of upset."

TWELVE

*U*pset? Upset?" Sir Hops-A-Lot worried, his nose hidden in a clump of still green grass.

"Yes, I have to be the Sugar Plum Princess and learn *thousands* of lines, and worst of all," she paused dramatically, *"I'll have to sing the lullaby. All alone."*

"Oh, dear," Miss Sassy Tail repeated, standing on her hind legs to peer into Chantelle's downcast face.

"Too bad," Rusty Raccoon added. "Well, you could always…"

"Chantelle?" her mother called. "Come in and have some cocoa. Savannah's here. We're making Christmas cookies."

"You could always wear a mask like I do," Rusty Raccoon finished. "At least no one will recognize you."

Miss Sassy Tail jumped from the gazebo to the tree as Chantelle disappeared into the house. "You weren't much help," she scolded Sir Hops-A-Lot.

"I don't know anything about singing," Sir Hops-A-Lot defended himself.

"Humph," Miss Sassy Tail sniffed, dashing up the tree. "And you!" she accused Rusty Raccoon. "A mask, indeed!"

"I thought it was a very good idea," the bushy raccoon asserted.

"Chantelle doesn't need ideas. She needs, she needs…" Miss Sassy Tail was leaping from branch to branch, heading for the very tip top of the exceedingly tall tree.

"Sympathy?" Sir Hops-A-Lot supplied softly.

"No, no, no! Not sympathy. She needs… CONFIDENCE!" And batting her long eyelashes, Miss Sassy Tail leaped, flying from the highest fork in the trunk out over the spreading limbs almost to the ground, reaching for and grabbing the very last branch, twisting nearly upside down, then deftly pulling herself upright. With a tiny shake, she smoothed her ruffled fur and straightened her hat. Looking to her friends, she held their attention with a proud smile. "Confidence, my dears, confidence."

ut honey, I thought you were excited about the play," Chantelle's mother said, cutting a gingerbread man from the brown sheet of cookie dough.

Chantelle took a sip of cocoa. "Well, I was, but..."

"But what?"

"But I didn't think I would have to be the Sugar Plum Princess!"

"But this is perfect!" Savannah exclaimed. "*You're* going to be the Sugar Plum Princess and *I'm* going to be the Christmas Angel!" She grabbed Chantelle's hands and twirled around the kitchen, dragging her friend with her, only coming to a stop when she realized Chantelle wasn't nearly so excited herself. "You don't look very happy about it," she finally said. "Don't you want to be the Princess?"

"No," Chantelle said, shaking her head.

Her mother bent down to hug them both. "The Sugar Plum Princess is a wonderful part. You'll be wearing a beautiful dress and you'll carry the magic wand..."

"But, Mother," Chantelle said, "the Sugar Plum Princess has to sing. All alone. What if everybody laughs at me?"

Chantelle's mother hugged her daughter again. "No one is going to laugh at you, dear. You have a very pretty singing voice. It's just a little quiet."

"That's because I don't want anyone to hear me," Chantelle mumbled into her mother's shoulder. "Besides, what if I forget the words? The Sugar Plum Princess has about a *million* lines..."

FIFTEEN

We'll practice together!" shouted Savannah, eager to cheer her friend. "Practice and practice and..."

"That's right. You can do anything if you think you can. You just need confidence. And the way to become confident is to practice." She gave Savannah an extra squeeze. "Come on, girls. Let's start right now. Who knows a really good Christmas carol?"

"I do, I do, I do!" yelled Savannah, climbing up on her stool. "The one about Rudolph! I love reindeer!"

Chantelle's mother started the song as she carefully cut out gingerbread men.

Soon Chantelle was so busy sprinkling colored candies onto gingerbread men that she forgot that she was singing. Forgot, that is, until she realized she was singing all alone. When her mother and Savannah started applauding, Chantelle hung her head sheepishly.

"We knew you could do it!" Savannah proclaimed happily. "You're going to be the best Sugar Plum Princess ever!"

other says I need confidence," Chantelle told Miss Sassy Tail. "And Savannah thinks I need practice."

"And what do *you* think you need?" Miss Sassy Tail asked. It was nearly twilight and they were sitting in the gazebo watching for the first twinkling stars.

"A different part in the Christmas Play," Chantelle answered, then laughed a tinkling laugh. "No, I'll be the Sugar Plum Princess, but I don't think I will be a very good one," she added.

"Hmmmm," Miss Sassy Tail said, stepping back a little and balancing on her hind feet. "You *look* like a Sugar Plum Princess," she said finally.

"I just don't sound like one," Chantelle pointed out.

"Well, of course, I wouldn't know about that, since I've never heard you sing," Miss Sassy Tail replied, thoughtfully. "Why don't you sing something?"

"Is anybody listening?" Chantelle whispered.

"Well, of course, we're *all* listening!" Miss Sassy Tail said indignantly.

"Sorry." Chantelle smoothed her hand down the squirrel's back. "I meant people."

"Oh, well, no, I don't suppose there are any of *those* around." Miss Sassy Tail jumped to the gazebo railing, becoming an eager audience. "You may begin," she encouraged, standing up and crossing her tiny grey-brown paws over her chest, waiting.

Chantelle burst out laughing. "Right now?"

Miss Sassy Tail nodded solemnly.

"Oh, no, I could not do that, not just stand up and sing."

"Of course you can! The Sugar Plum Princess *has* to sing," Miss Sassy Tail insisted. When Chantelle only shook her head, the perky little squirrel leaped to her shoulder and whispered into her ear. "Shall I tell you a secret?" she asked softly. "I *know* that you can sing."

Chantelle wasn't nearly as convinced. Darting her eyes to the sky, she saw it: the first star. "I win!"

"And what is your wish?" Miss Sassy Tail asked very seriously.

"Please," Chantelle whispered aloud, "please don't let me ruin the Christmas Play."

NINETEEN

TWENTY

*T*he night before the dress rehearsal, Chantelle and Savannah stepped carefully through the frosted grass, making their way to the gazebo. Miss Sassy Tail, Sir Hops-A-Lot, Rusty Raccoon and a great many others were waiting.

"Now, are you comfortable? Warm enough?" The diminutive squirrel fussed, then sat back on her slender haunches. "Whenever you're ready," she invited.

Holding Savannah's hand tightly, Chantelle took a deep breath and began the Sugar Plum Princess's lullaby to all the children of the world...

> *"Hush-a-bye, go to sleep,*
> *for the eve-ning is wa-ning,*
> *you'll be safe, in God's keep,*
> *slumber deep my dears, so sweet..."*

Mesmerized, Chantelle's friends were caught in the magic of her efforts, knowing how difficult it was. When Chantelle's voice quavered and Savannah joined in, not one pair of their brown eyes left her face.

> *"Hush-a-bye, and good-night,*
> *Christmas morn-ing will come soon,*
> *hush-a-bye, and good-night,*
> *go to sleep my dears, good-night."*

Sir Hops-A-Lot blinked away a glistening tear. "Extraordinary," he murmured.

"Oh, my, yes!" Miss Sassy Tail agreed enthusiastically. "Just splendid!"

"Did you really like it?" Chantelle asked hesitantly.

"My dear," Rusty Raccoon exclaimed, "you were marvelous! I take my hat off to you!" And to prove his point, he reached a black paw to the top of his head and snatched off his hat.

"Thank you," Chantelle said to the gallant raccoon. "You've made me feel so much better."

"Girls?" her mother called. "It's time for bed."

"Coming!" Savannah shouted.

"Thanks again," Chantelle called to her friends as they raced to the house.

hantelle's mother arrived early for the dress rehearsal and took a seat in the very first row.

The Christmas Play began in Santa's workshop. Frosty the Snowman and Rudolph the Red-Nosed Reindeer stood just behind the workshop windows where the audience could see them.

The chorus of Elves was busily singing while all the Christmas Bells jingled and jangled. They were readying Santa's sleigh on the night before Christmas when the news came over a special radio broadcast that no child anywhere in the world would be able to sleep on Christmas Eve. It was a wicked plot to keep Santa from delivering presents to all good children.

Chantelle, as the Sugar Plum Princess, was to break the spell with her lullaby.

When Chantelle appeared on stage, she was frightened. Nervously twisting her wand, she could hardly be heard. Her mother was smiling, trying to encourage her, but when Chantelle faltered during the lullaby, Mrs. Barnsworth called for a break.

While the other children stretched and chattered, Chantelle tiptoed across the stage to her mother. Mrs. Barnsworth joined them.

"You're doing just beautifully, Chantelle," Mrs. Barnsworth assured her.

"Yes, you are," her mother added. "I'm so proud of you."

"But, I think you might find it easier if you sing a bit louder," Mrs. Barnsworth said.

"Imagine that I am in the back row," her mother said, "and you have to sing loud enough that I can hear you."

"Let's try it one more time," Mrs. Barnsworth suggested.

TWENTY-THREE

TWENTY-FOUR

The night of the Play, Savannah and Chantelle stood behind the purple stage curtains, looking for their parents. Savannah found hers right away. "Look, there they are!" But Chantelle was still looking for hers. She couldn't find them.

The auditorium was filling up with hundreds of people... and her mother and father were not to be seen!

Mrs. Barnsworth came up behind her and spoke quietly. "Chantelle, I just spoke with your mother on the telephone. They're going to be a little late."

Chantelle whirled around, her eyes opened very wide.

"They're on their way now," Mrs. Barnsworth said quickly, "but they may have to stand in the back."

"They won't hear me back there!" Chantelle exclaimed.

Mrs. Barnsworth nodded. "You'll have to sing very loudly," she said, "but I know you can do it! You've practiced and practiced. You know all your lines and you know the song. This is your night to prove it to yourself," she said. "You're going to be wonderful!"

When Chantelle stepped on stage, she tried to see to the back of the auditorium, but the bright stage lights were shining in her eyes.

As she turned to ask Rudolph to fetch Santa, she saw Mrs. Barnsworth backstage. "They're here," Mrs. Barnsworth whispered.

As Chantelle began, her only thought was to sing to her mother, far away in the back of the auditorium. She sang louder and stronger than she had ever sung.

ith her sweet, clear voice filling the crowded auditorium, the Elves on stage pretended to fall asleep. The Christmas Bells jangled as they dropped into a drowsy heap, then Frosty nodded his head, sleepily.

Even Savannah, as the Christmas Angel, covered a yawn. Santa climbed into his present-laden sleigh ready for his Christmas deliveries as she sang the very last line.

"Thank you, Sugar Plum Princess," he called. "Merry Christmas to you, and Merry Christmas to all!"

As Chantelle and Savannah took their bows, the thundering waves of applause surprised Chantelle so much that she had to smile. The Christmas Play was a magical success!

"Did you see her laugh?" Miss Sassy Tail chattered excitedly.

"Don't they look beautiful?" Sir Hops-A-Lot murmured in awe.

Absolutely captivated, Rusty Raccoon declared, "I wouldn't have missed it for the world!"

After the last curtain call, Savannah hugged her friend. "Didn't I tell you?" she demanded happily as they changed into party dresses. "You can do anything that you want to do."

"It was all our practicing that did it," Chantelle admitted. "Thank you for believing in me, Savannah!"

And she clasped a gold friendship necklace around Savannah's neck. Inscribed on the heart half was the word "Friends". With a hug, Chantelle showed her own necklace to Savannah. Her half of the heart read "Forever".

"Merry Christmas, Savannah!"

"Merry Christmas, Chantelle!"

And a very Merry Christmas to you!

The Magical World of Storybook Heirlooms

Chantelle's adventures are just part of the enchanting world of Storybook Heirlooms. For girls just like you, it is a catalogue filled with wonderful clothes and charming accessories that you can wear, from exquisite old-fashioned party gowns to comfortable sportswear for every day. You can meet our beautiful Chantelle doll, whose wardrobe matches many outfits found in the Storybook catalogue. And in our Sticker Paper Doll series, you can follow the fun as Chantelle and her adorable friends Elizabeth and Savannah romp at a ranch, have a tea party, and much more!

To visit the magical world of Storybook Heirlooms, complete this postcard and mail it to us. We will send you a catalogue filled with delightful timeless clothing and gifts for girls.

To receive a Storybook Heirlooms catalogue,
please fill out the postcard below,
or call toll-free **1-800-825-6565**.

Please send me a Storybook Catalogue

Please send a catalogue to:

Name: _____

Address: _____

City/State/Zip: _____

_____

Send a catalogue to a friend:

Name: _____

Address: _____

City/State/Zip: _____

_____

Or Call Toll Free 1-800-825-6565

Key 50-825

PLACE
STAMP
HERE

333 Hatch Dr
Foster City CA 94404-1162